la-la!

by Karen Beaumont

illustrated by LeUyen Pham

Scholastic Press
New York

Party dresses, party hair . . .
Need new party shoes to wear.
Emily, Ashley, Kaitlyn, Claire!
Let's go find the perfect pair!

Shoe-la-la!

They're *everywhere.*

Rows and rows!

These or those?

Up, up on our tippy toes.

Can't wait to choose new shoes.

Here goes!

Shoes with zippers,

Shoes with straps,

Shoes with buckles,

Shoes with taps.

Shoes with laces, shoes with bows,

Sorry, sir. We *don't* like those. They hurt our toes.

I'll try on this rainbow pair.

Hey! These match my underwear!

Lots and lots of leopard spots.

Pink and purple polka dots.

These show off
my pretty feet.

These look good
enough to eat.

Fuzzy boots for
when it snows.

Ballerina
on my toes!

Cowgirl . . .

Rock star . . .

Princess . . .

Bride . . .

This pair? That pair? Can't decide.

Fancy ribbons,
   Frilly lace.
Shoe-la-la!
   We *love* this place!

Sparkly diamonds, pretty pearls,
Ritzy, glitzy

Uh-oh!
Store's about to close!
Which shoes
should we choose—
who knows?

Emily,
Ashley,
Kaitlyn,
Claire!
Hurry, hurry!
Pick a pair!

Piles and piles
fill the aisles.

Never seen
so many styles.

Shop and shop until we drop!
Guess it's time for us to STOP!

Eeny, meeny, my oh my!
Just don't know which shoes to buy.

Can't decide. We've seen too many.

Sorry, sir.
We *don't* want ANY!

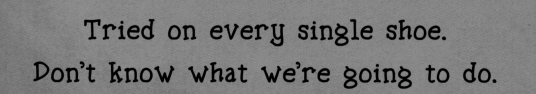

Tried on every single shoe.
Don't know what we're going to do.

Party dresses,

Party hair . . .

Perfect party shoes to wear!

For my daughters, Christina and Nicolyn.
I love you with all of my heart . . . and "sole"!
—K.B.

To Kay, the ultimate Shoe-Gal.
—L.P.

Beaumont, Karen.
Shoe-la-la! / by Karen Beaumont ; illustrated by LeUyen Pham.   p. cm.
Summary: Four girls go in search of the perfect pair of party shoes.
ISBN 978-0-545-06705-8 (hardcover : alk. paper)
[1. Stories in rhyme. 2. Shoes — Fiction.] I. Pham, LeUyen, ill. II. Title.
PZ8.3.B3845Sh 2011   [E] — dc22   2010007848

10 9 8 7 6 5 4 3 2   11 12 13 14 15
Printed in China   62
First edition, January 2011

The text was set in Spellstone.
Book design by Lillie Howard